∵ *A Book of Lullabies* ∾

DREAMTIME

selected by Belinda Hollyer
illustrated by Robin Bell Corfield

VIKING

the evening is coming

The evening is coming, the sun sinks to rest,
The birds are all flying straight home to their nests,
"Caw, caw," says the crow as he flies overhead,
It's time little children were going to bed.

Here comes the pony, his work is all done,
Down through the meadow he takes a good run,
Up go his heels—and down goes his head,
It's time little children were going to bed.

bedtime

Five minutes, five minutes more please!
  Let me stay five minutes more!
Can't I just finish the castle
  I'm building here on the floor?
Can't I just finish the story
  I'm reading here in my book?
Can't I just finish this bead-chain—
  It *almost* is finished, look!
Can't I just finish this game please?
  When a game's once begun
It's a pity never to find out
  Whether you've lost or won.
Can't I just stay five minutes?
  Well, can't I stay just four?
Three minutes then? two minutes?
  Can't I stay just *one* minute more?

~ *Eleanor Farjeon* ~

go to bed, tom

Go to bed, Tom,
Go to bed, Tom,
Tired or not, Tom.
Go to bed, Tom.

getting-ready-lullaby

Hug me gentle, hug me strong,
hug me short and hug me long.
Now it's time to put away
all the pieces of today—
all the games and all the toys,
all the bother and the noise,
all the girls and all the boys—
back they go into their box
till tomorrow morning knocks.

Now a bath for sleepyhead,
then it's story time in bed,
then once more it's hug-me-tight,
kisses, and turn out the light.

∴ *Russell Hoban* ∴

down with the lambs

Down with the lambs,
Up with the lark,
Run to bed children
Before it gets dark.

go to bed late

Go to bed late,
Stay very small;
Go to bed early,
Grow very tall.

i see the moon

I see the moon
And the moon sees me;
God bless the moon
And God bless me.

in jumping and tumbling

In jumping and tumbling
We spend the whole day,
Till night by arriving
Has finished our play.

What then? One and all,
There's no more to be said,
As we tumbled all day,
So we tumble to bed.

you be saucer

You be saucer,
I'll be cup,
piggyback, piggyback
pick me up.

You be tree,
I'll be pears,
carry me, carry me
up the stairs.

You be Good,
I'll be Night,
tuck me in, tuck me in
nice and tight.

⌒∴ *Eve Merriam* ∴⌒

ten, nine, eight

10 small toes all washed and warm
 9 soft friends in a quiet room
 8 square windowpanes with falling snow
 7 empty shoes in a short straight row
 6 pale seashells hanging down
 5 round buttons on a yellow gown
 4 sleepy eyes which open and close
 3 loving kisses on cheeks and nose
 2 strong arms around a fuzzy bear's head
 1 big girl all ready for bed

⌣ *Molly Bang* ⌣

good night

Now good night.
  Fold up your clothes
  As you were taught,
  Fold your two hands,
  Fold up your thought;
  Day is the plough-land,
  Night is the stream,
  Day is for doing
  And night is for dream.
Now good night.

⌣ *Eleanor Farjeon* ⌣

god bless this house from thatch to floor

God bless this house from thatch to floor,
The twelve apostles guard the door.
Four angels to my bed;
Gabriel stands at the head,
John and Peter at my feet,
All to watch me while I sleep.

dance to your daddy

Dance to your daddy
My little babby,
Dance to your daddy
My little lamb

You shall have a fishy
In a little dishy,
You shall have a fishy
When the boat comes in.

hushabye my darling

Hushabye my darling
Don't you make a peep
Little creatures everywhere
Are settling down to sleep

Fishes in the millpond
Goslings in the barn
Kitten by the fireside
Baby in my arms

Listen to the raindrops
Singing you to sleep
Hushabye my darling
Don't you make a peep

Clyde Watson

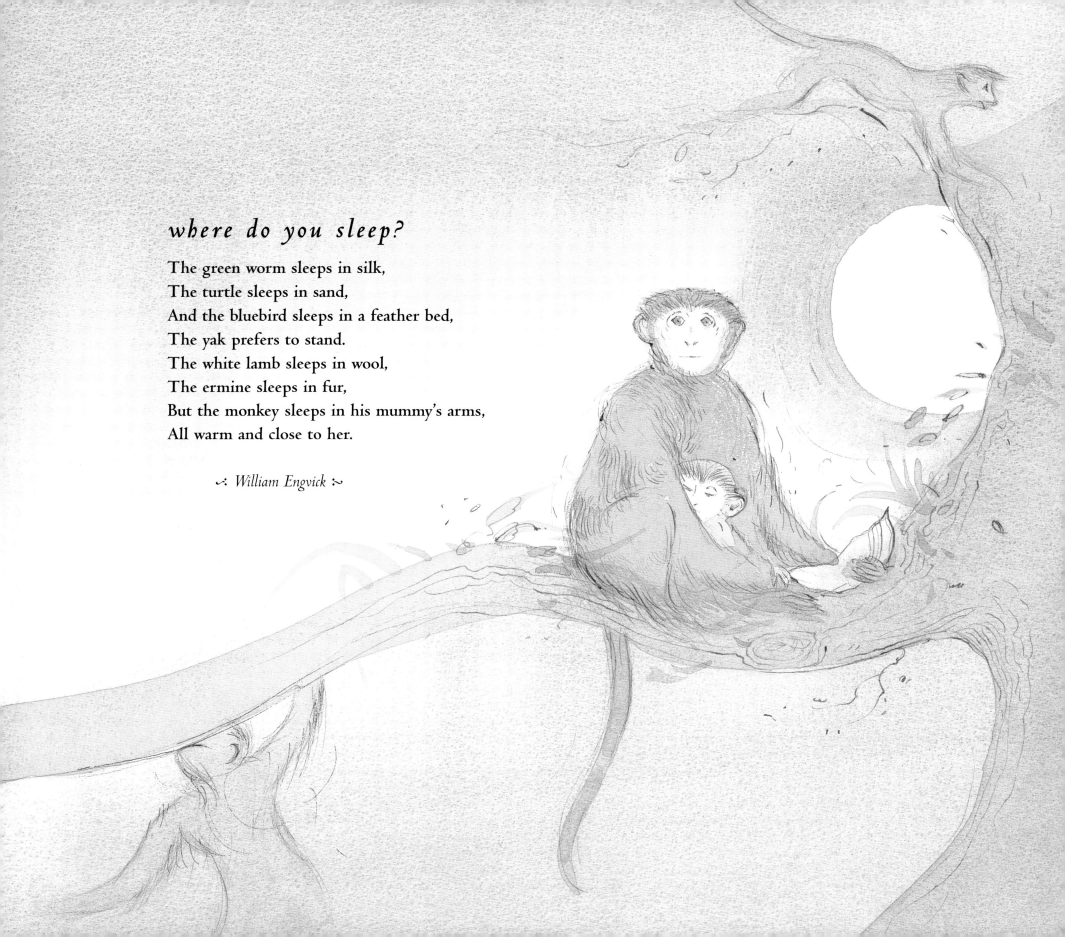

where do you sleep?

The green worm sleeps in silk,
The turtle sleeps in sand,
And the bluebird sleeps in a feather bed,
The yak prefers to stand.
The white lamb sleeps in wool,
The ermine sleeps in fur,
But the monkey sleeps in his mummy's arms,
All warm and close to her.

William Engvick

dream-song

Sunlight, moonlight,
Twilight, starlight—
Gloaming at the close of day,
And an owl calling,
Cool dews falling
In a wood of oak and may.

Lantern-light, taper-light,
Torchlight, no-light:
Darkness at the shut of day,
And lions roaring,
Their wrath pouring
In wild waste places far away.

Elf-light, bat-light,
Touchwood-light and toad-light
And the sea a shimmering gloom of grey,
And a small face smiling
In a dream's beguiling
In a world of wonders far away.

∴ *Walter de la Mare* ∴

the mother sings

Rockaby, my baby,
Slumber if you can.
I wonder what you're going to be
When you're grown a man.

If you are a monarch
On a gold and silver throne,
With all the lands of East and West
For to call your own,
I know you'll be the greatest monarch
Ever was known.

If you are poet
With the magic of the word,
A swan's quill to write with
And a voice like a bird,
I know you'll be the greatest poet
Ever was heard.

But whether you're a monarch
And make your bride a queen,
Or whether you're a poet
With men's hearts to glean,
I know you are the sweetest baby
Ever was seen.

Rockaby, my baby,
Slumber if you can.
I wonder what you're going to be
When you're grown a man.

~: *Eleanor Farjeon* :~

gaelic lullaby

Hush! the waves are rolling in,
  White with foam, white with foam;
Father toils amid the din;
  But baby sleeps at home.

Hush! the winds roar hoarse and deep,
  On they come, on they come!
Brother seeks the wandering sheep;
  But baby sleeps at home.

Hush! the rain sweeps over the knowes,
  Where they roam, where they roam;
Sister goes to seek the cows;
  But baby sleeps at home.

oh father's at the sea

Oh father's at the sea,
  baby mine,
Oh father's at the sea,
  baby mine,
And you're all I've got,
Here asleeping in your cot,
  Such a blessed little dot,
  baby mine.

∴ *Thomas E. Brown* ∴

the sounds in the evening

The sounds in the evening
Go all through the house,
The click of the clock
And the pick of the mouse,
The footsteps of people
Upon the top floor,
The skirts of my mother
That brush by my door,
The crick in the boards,
And the creak of the chairs,
The fluttering murmurs
Outside on the stairs,
The ring at the bell,
The arrival of guests,
The laugh of my father
At one of his jests,
The clashing of dishes
As dinner goes in,
The babble of voices
That distance makes thin,
The mewings of cats
That seem just by my ear,
The hooting of owls
That can never seem near,
The queer little noises
That no one explains—
Till the moon through the slats
Of my window-blind rains,
And the world of my eyes
And my ears melts like steam
As I find in my pillow
The world of my dream.

◡: *Eleanor Farjeon* :◡

night sounds

In the street
  sounds of wheels humming,
  sounds of heels drumming.
Humming and drumming,
Keeping me from sleeping.
In the house
  sounds of words mumbling,
  overhead grumbling.
Mumbling and grumbling,
Keeping me unsleeping.
Far away
  sounds of waves lashing,
  quietly crashing.
Lashing and crashing,
Sweeping me to sleep.

∴ *Felice Holman* ∵

evening

Hush, hush, little baby,
  The sun's in the west;
The lamb in the meadow
  Has laid down to rest.

The bough rocks the bird now,
  The flower rocks the bee,
The waves rocks the lily,
  The wind rocks the tree;

And I rock the baby
  So softly to sleep—
It must not awaken
  Till daisy-buds peep.

lullaby

The moon and the stars and the wind in the sky
All night long sing a lullaby,
While down in the ocean so dark and so deep
The silvery waves rock the fishes to sleep.

∴ *Jean Jaszi* ∴

all tucked in & roasty toasty

All tucked in & roasty toasty
Blow me a kiss good-night
Close your eyes till morning comes
Happy dreams & sleep tight.

∴ Clyde Watson ∴

are all the giants dead?

Are all the giants dead?
And all the witches fled?
Am I quite safe in bed?

Giants and witches all are fled.
My child, thou art quite safe in bed.

a spell for sleeping

Sweet william, silverweed, sally-my-handsome.
Dimity darkens the pittering water.
On gloomed lawns wanders a king's daughter.
Curtains are clouding the casement windows.
A moon-glade smurrs the lake with light.
Doves cover the tower with quiet.

Three owls whit-whit in the withies.
Seven fish in a deep pool shimmer.
The princess moves to the spiral stair.

Slowly the sickle moon mounts up.
Frogs hump under moss and mushroom.
The princess climbs to her high hushed room,

Step by step to her shadowed tower.
Water laps the white lake shore.
A ghost opens the princess' door.

Seven fish in the sway of the water.
Six candles for a king's daughter.
Five sighs for a drooping head.
Four ghosts to gentle her bed.
Three owls in the dusk falling.
Two tales to be telling.
One spell for sleeping.

Tamarisk, trefoil, tormentil.
Sleep rolls down from the clouded hill.
A princess dreams of a silver pool.

The moonlight spreads, the soft ferns flitter.
Stilled in a shimmering drift of water,
Seven fish dream of a lost king's daughter.

∽ *Alastair Reid* ∽

once, a lullaby

Once I was a little horse,
baby horse, little horse.
Once I was a little horse.
Neigh, I fell asleep.

Once I was a little cow,
baby cow, little cow.
Once I was a little cow.
Moo, I fell asleep

Once I was a little goat,
baby goat, little goat.
Once I was a little goat.
Maa, I fell asleep.

Once I was a little sheep,
baby sheep, little sheep.
Once I was a little sheep.
Baa, I fell asleep.

Once I was a little dog,
baby dog, little dog.
One I was a little dog.
Arf, I fell asleep.

Once I was a little owl,
baby owl, little owl.
Once I was a little owl.
Whoo, I went to sleep.

And then:
Bee—*bzzz*
Boy—*waa*
Chick—*cheep*
Crow—*caw*
Duck—*quack*
Fish—*glub*
Fly—*hmmm*
Frog—*croak*
Girl—*waa*

∼: *bp Nichol* :∼

Once I was a little mouse,
baby mouse, little mouse.
Once I was a little mouse.
Squeak, I went to sleep.

lullaby

Sh   sh   what do you wish
sh   sh   the windows are shuttered
sh   sh   a magical fish
swims out from the window and down to the river

lap   lap   the waters are lapping
sh   sh   the shore slips away
glide glide glide with the current
sh   sh   the shadows are deeper

sleep   sleep   tomorrow is sure

‿∴ *Eve Merriam* ∵‿

pillow song

Moony, moony, silver deep
Ocean rock me to my sleep
Morning sunshine in my cup
Sing a song to wake me up.

∾ *Russell Hoban* ∾

catch me the moon, daddy

Catch me the moon, Daddy,
Let it shine near me for a while,
Catch me the moon, Daddy,
I want to touch its smile.

The moon must shine from high above;
That's where it needs to stay
Among the stars, to guide them home
When they return from play.

So the bunny can find his supper,
So the mouse can scamper free,
So the hedgehog can make his forays,
So the birds can sleep in the tree.

And as for you, my child,
With slender silver thread
The moon will weave sweet dreams, so you
May slumber in your bed.

‿ *Grigor Vitez* ⁖

the white seal's lullaby

Oh! hush thee, my baby, the night is behind us,
  And black are the waters that sparkled so green.
The moon, o'er the combers, looks downward to find us
  At rest in the hollows that rustle between.
Where billow meets billow, then soft be thy pillow;
  Ah, weary wee flipperling, curl at thy ease!
The storm shall not wake thee, nor shark overtake thee,
  Asleep in the arms of the slow-swinging seas.

❦ *Rudyard Kipling* ❧

VIKING
Published by the Penguin Group
Penguin Putnam Inc., 375 Hudson Street, New York, New York 10014, U.S.A.
Penguin Books Ltd, 27 Wrights Lane, London W8 5TZ, England
Penguin Books Australia Ltd, Ringwood, Victoria, Australia
Penguin Books Canada Ltd, 10 Alcorn Avenue, Toronto, Ontario, Canada M4V 3B2
Penguin Books (N.Z.) Ltd, 182-190 Wairau Road, Auckland 10, New Zealand

Penguin Books Ltd, Registered Offices: Harmondsworth, Middlesex, England

First published in Great Britain by Bloomsbury Publishing Plc, 1998
Published in the United States by Viking, a member of Penguin Putnam Books for Young Readers, 1999

1 3 5 7 9 10 8 6 4 2

ISBN 0-670-88363-8
Library of Congress Catalog Card Number: 98-60929

Printed in Singapore
Set in Centaur